• Alyssa Satin Capucilli •

Tulip Loves Rex

• Illustrated by Sarah Massini •

KATHERINE TEGEN BOOKS
An Imprint of HarperCollins Publishers

Katherine Tegen Books is an imprint of HarperCollins Publishers.

Tulip Loves Rex
Text copyright © 2014 by Alyssa Satin Capucilli
Illustrations copyright © 2014 by Sarah Massini
All rights reserved. Manufactured in China.

Library of Congress Cataloging-in-Publication Data is available.
ISBN 978-0-06-209413-1

The artist used mixed traditional media and Photoshop to create the digital illustrations for this book.
Designed by Martha Rago
13 14 15 16 17   SCP   10 9 8 7 6 5 4 3 2 1
❖
First Edition

For Peter and Laura, with love
—A.S.C.

For Sophie
—S.M.

From the very moment she was born, Tulip
loved to dance.
    While the other babies were learning to crawl,
Tulip was ready to spin.

While some toddlers said "Mama" and "Dada" and even "goo," Tulip's first words were "whirl" and "twirl" and "leap"!

Her parents looked at each other. Tulip was not quite like other children. They didn't mind a bit.

Tulip grew and grew.
Her dancing grew, too.

Tulip greeted every morning with a graceful gallop and a cheerful skip.

And in the evening, when she sent her wish-upon-the-stars,
it was always the very same wish, off with a bend and a sway.
It seemed the very best way.
Tulip loved to dance!

One spring day, Tulip skipped outside in the gentle
morning sun. She balanced on one leg.

She leaped over puddles great and wide.

Her parents looked at each other. Was there anyone
who loved to dance as much as Tulip?

Tulip galloped.

Tulip curtsied to the smiling flowers.

And then, Tulip stopped.

There was a dog.

It was a rather large
dog. The dog wore a sign
around its neck.

My name is
REX
I am not
quite like
other dogs

Tulip looked at her parents. Her parents looked at Rex. Rex licked Tulip's cheek.

"I'm sure that's the happiest lick anyone has ever given me," said Tulip. It made her want to hop!

"Here now, Rex," said Tulip.
"Let's see what you can do."

Tulip threw a stick. "Fetch it,
Rex," she said.
Rex scratched his ear.

Tulip tossed a ball to Rex.
"Can you catch it, Rex?"
Rex only yawned.

"Sit, Rex, sit," said Tulip.
Rex rolled onto his back.

"Hmm," said Tulip, folding her arms. "I guess
you aren't quite like other dogs, are you, Rex?"
Rex covered his eye with his paw!

"That's okay, Rex," said Tulip. "I don't mind a
bit. We all have something we love to do. We just
have to discover what it is."

Tulip twirled. Twirling always helped
her think more clearly.
  "See, Rex? I love to dance," said Tulip.
Rex sat up and barked.

Tulip hopped up

and down

and up

and down.

Rex wagged his tail.

Tulip spun wildly about with her arms stretched wide.

Now Rex spun wildly about, too. He barked and wagged his tail again and again. "Oh, Rex," said Tulip. "Could it be? I don't suppose you love to dance, too?" Rex licked Tulip's cheek once more!

Tulip and Rex galloped through the soft grass.
They spun in circles around the trees.

They leaped after spotted butterflies until
Tulip's parents called, "It's time to go home, Tulip."

Tulip hugged Rex tightly. She buried her face
in his soft, soft ears.

"You may not be quite like other dogs, Rex,
but I think you are the very best dog in the world.
I love to dance, Rex. And I love you, too."

Tulip twirled good-bye
to Rex. She did a cartwheel.

She stood on her head.
And that's when she saw it!

"Wait," said Tulip.
"Could it be . . . ?"

Rex barked. He wagged his tail again and again.

"You're right, Rex," said Tulip. "Standing on your head gives you a whole new way of looking at things, doesn't it?"

Now Tulip looked at her parents. Rex looked, too.
"Can we take Rex home?" asked Tulip. "Please?"
Tulip's parents looked at each other.

A rather large dog named
Rex who loved to dance?
They didn't mind a bit!

That evening, Tulip stood by her window. "Thank you," she whispered to the stars, with an extra-big bend and an extra-special sway. After all, that was the very best way.

"It seems wishes come in all shapes and sizes," said Tulip, "quite like love."

Tulip loved to dance. Tulip loved Rex, too.

"But there's nothing quite like sharing love, is there, Rex?" Tulip said, yawning with a sleepy twirl.

Rex curled up by Tulip's bed. He wagged
his tail, a bit sleepily, to the stars, too.

He loved to dance. He loved Tulip.
He loved being loved most of all.